Bounty

I fired one-single-shot.

The creature I hit lay lifeless in the poison fog ahead. I made sure my fog mask was on correctly before going to retrieve the carcass I hit. As I walked toward the creature, I thought to myself, "Another bounty I would collect to put food in my belly".

Who am I? Well, I'm not the average teenage girl. I'm Sarah. I don't have a family, a bed or any of those 29th century comforts most girls my age have. I'm a young techno punk girl. But. I do have my bike and my robot. Yeah, I said robot; its last thing you would expect a 16 year old girl would have. In fact, most girls my age would find that weird. That's not all that's so called weird about me. I learned fairly quickly in my youth that my eyes changes color; not a super rarer thing to poses, it doesn't make me super special but, it is unique. Oh and you know now, that I kill for a living. I am a 16 year old teenage bounty hunter; now that is something you don't see very often.

And. That makes me special. A RARERTY. I reached for the carcass of the demon like animal I killed with a single shot and dragged it over to my bike where my prized DSREP rifle lay. I dropped the animal and grabbed my rifle, pressed a lit button on the top of my techno gauntlet1 and let it do its thing.

Bounty

The gauntlet emitted a blue light that covered my rife then flattened it into a 2-D plain. The blue light triggers the weapon to fold and insert itself into slot NO.1 of my gauntlet attached to my left forearm. I then summoned Jipsy, my trusty robot to carry the carcass back up to the city. “Good afternoon Sarah” said Jipsy. “Was your hunt successful?” he asked. “Yeah,Yeah skip the chatter and just carry this for me while we head off to the city.” I responded while I picked up the animal and threw it at him. He immediately picked it up with his antimatter field and was ready to pursuit me immediately. I mounted my vintage electric blue anti mater motorbike that I stole from some punk gang a few years ago. I started the AI, which greeted me with a monotone voice, “Ready” and I headed up to the city in the sky with Jispy following me faithfully.

As we approached the city, I removed my oxygen mask and requested that Jipsy stay close. You never know what happens in this city, one thing I know for sure is thing happen up here. One moment you could be shopping and then, BOOM! Your dead as a door nail. We hurried swiftly to my usual dealer, Quavo’ a *Sartarian. Quaco’* only talks business and pays fairly decent. “Shall I communicate to Quavo’ that we are close” Asked Jipsy.

Bounty

“You know Jispy, you don’t have to ask me for such commands after every hunt, we do this all the time after a hunt; there is no need to ask my permission to contact Quavo’ each time.” I exclaimed annoyingly. “Yes, we do, but I need to make sure that the command is final.” Responded Jipsy. “Yeah yeah whatever.” I snarled back.

We landed on the city in the sky and headed straight to Quavo’s place. As usual the front entrance was cluttered with a bunch of punks that think to highly of themselves. As we approached, I could tell the punks hanging out by Quavo’s shack were sizing me up. No doubt they sized me up to be a sweet young thing without the ability to protect myself. One guy, the tallest of them all, anticipated no resistance on my part or he wouldn’t had jumped to approach me. Tall guy rushed to me as I approached the front entrance of Quavo’s place and asked for my code. Instinctively, I upholstered a small carving knife from my right thigh like an automatic reflex you would have if an unfounded object approached you at a dangerous speed. I held it tight to his neck in moments, pushing against his pail white skin. The blade scratched his neck as I pressed against it. “What did you say?” I sternly asked. Within seconds and to no surprise to me, he backed off. Typical punk, thinking he pray on weak young females. Not this time, I am far from weak.

Bounty

I suppose there are countless punks in this city that would see a pretty young girl like me and assume I am meek and an easy prey; demand for my code. The least he could do is try and get to know a girl-date her- you know- crap like that. If you can't already tell, I don't have an interest in guys. I'm only interested in things that keep me alive in this cruel world; my bike and my gauntlet, they keep me alive and moving. I told Jipsy to wait for me around back. Quavo' has a strict no bot policy and I don't want to get on his bad side again. I pushed my way through the metallic, ancient looking door and made my way to the bar area filled with drunk slobs and waitress begging for tips. It discussed me and it smelled of liquor and sweat. I passed the bar area and entered a small room behind the staff. Quavo stood at attention upon directly in my line of sight as he greeted me with a long drawl like twang in his voice. "Awwww look what we have here, pretty young bounty hunter. What are the spoils this time?" "Just a feline Avdero, a nice one too, if I do say so myself." It's out back if you're wondering." I said steadily as I gestured towards the back door. "Then what are we waiting for, let us see." Echoed Quavo. He made his way through dozens of artifacts and bounties he already collected from other hunters. I followed him as he pushed open the back door and walked out of his establishment.

Bounty

Jipsy, was floating there motionless awaiting my commands. “Turn off the field.” I instructed Jipsy. The feline Avdero fell to the ground with a thump and Jipsy made its way to my AI. Just like any other transaction, Jipsy did not say a word. It’s not like he was scared or anything, I just demand he shut off his enquiry mode and let me do business. Quavo examined the creature, picking up its tail, checking its teeth and groping every inch of the dead carcass. Finally he looked up at me and gave me a number; “4,200” he screeched. “4,500” I replied. He counter with another low ball number and I countered with “4,300?.... yes?” I thought about it for a moment. Usually he has a fair price to offer, I opened my mouth to speak again but- he cut me off. “A girl like you doesn't get much appreciation you know; I’m the only Satarian alive that would think of dealing with a human like you.” His voice sounding deeper now. He's actually right; I literally am the only human who deals with Quavo. Most of his dealers are off worlder drug smugglers and quick money maker scam artist. “4,300 credits it is.” He bellowed as we shook on it. We headed on in with a fair deal, a respectable deal, a real deal. I can’t tell you how many times I’ve been robbed by people that have some radar thing that credits you and then retracts the credits. No, Quavo has always been a straighter up guy with me. I left the building and summoned Jipsy out of my gauntlet then started my bike.

Bounty

"Did the transaction go well Sarah?" Jipsy asked in the most innocent tone. "yeah yeah, I got 4300 for it" I smirked. "You know Sarah there are other things you can do besides bounty hunting" indicated Jipsy. "How many times do we have to go over this Jipsy, I do not care what other girls my age are doing. I about that stuff like that!" I furiously replied. I've stated that so many times and it seems like he can't get that through his thick motherboard that I don't care for those modern teen desirables or trinkets. I grew up differently and my lifestyle would not change-EVER.... Even if it did, I still wouldn't take advice from a robot.

Bounty

I took a minute to shrug off Jipsy's comments. When I finally calmed down, I started my bike and brought up the AI display on my bike which shown the news and any new bounties up for grabs. I always pull them up after a pay day and lock in the next job with my ID. I noticed on the top of the list was a job that paid 6,000,000,000 credits. With no hesitation or thought at all, I inserted my ID and claimed the job as mine so no one can take it, then…. "UGGG!!!" I exclaimed out loud. I realized what I had done after reading the details of the job. I just signed myself up to assassinate an entire banned drug soliciting bunch of hooligans; an entire weapon and people smuggler gang down on the surface. This gang is ruthless and are highly trained killers, they have been doing this for longer than I've been alive. I literally can't believe that I signed myself up for something so hard to accomplish. I have the gear that is required to do this job, but, I have never faced multiple targets at one time. This job has been the top of the list for years. Every day the bounty gets bigger and larger. I wasn't tempted by greed, I would have seen that this job was the same job that's always on top. I was as mad and huffed around like a baby when its mom is away.

Bounty

I was seriously mad at myself. I couldn't help thinking crazy thoughts as I shouted "I'm better off dead than getting this bounty" I knew by law I had no choice but to do the job. I entered my ID and now I am stuck with this job. "I have to get it done as fast as I can" I thought to myself angrily. Steadying myself as well as I could, I nervously sent directions to my hover bike and it kicked into auto pilot then headed off in the direction of my next target, the banned drug soliciting bunch of hooligans. We traveled South East, it will be 108 miles to travel. Jispy and I had to travel quite a bit to get there! Knowing how much time that would take, I summoned Jipsy while steading pour course. I gave Jipsy my card and instructed him buy me something to eat. "Yes Sarah" obediently replied and flew away. Waiting for Jipsy to return gave me time to open my GPS and take a look at the gang's location. The holographic map appeared before me and I saw that there was a warehouse of some sort covered by a ton of trees at the gang's last known location. The hologram could not depict the entrance of their hide out, but from what I could tell there was some sort of path leading to their compound. As any sniper trained bounty hunter would do, I immediately looked for hills to take a good position behind, but found none. The warehouse is located dead center in the crest at the bottom of a hill.

Bounty

I pondered a bit before an idea came into mind. I should have thought of it earlier; I will use my sniper and sit at the top of the hill, I'll send Jipsy down to 3-D map the area and place some sensors in the ground.
I can just wait till there's movement, when someone trips the sensors it will appear ton my 3-D map. Then I could take a shot with my sniper at a safe distance. Or, if I want to go aggressive, I can take my RRS and bust down the door and just spray 'em all. Both are valid options, but I prefer the safe route Jipsy came back a few moments later with some random bowl of rice looking substance glazed with sauce. He handed the food and my card to me and asked "does this please your demands?" I replied with my standard "yeah, yeah" It was kind of hard to eat while speeding in the sky at 50 miles per hour, but I managed. I devoured the food as fast as I possibly could, I didn't want any of it to fly away. I threw the container out into the sky and Jispy quickly captured it with his anti mater field. The field crushed the bowl into tiny little particles which Jispy set free into the tail wind closing following us behind. I was going to tell Jipsy my thoughts about the plan, but I decided to wait until we got there. I used my techno gauntlet and put Jispy away, no use wasting his battery when he can hitch a ride with me.

Bounty

I looked at the speedometer and thought to myself "dam, I only traveled 10 miles…" another 100 to go!" At least I was out of the city and soaring across the sky vastly, which was getting darker by the minute. I decided let the autopilot take over and do its thing to go while I safely got some much needed sleep. The auto pilot would detect any danger and avoid any harm while I slept. I pressed another dimly lit button on the bike and the part of my bike that I sat on slowly collapsed inward and revealed an empty compartment beneath me, just my size. I accidently found this feature on my bike while taking it apart when I was stealing it from some gang a while back. I furnished the area with some soft feathers I collect while hunting a large bird like creature. I was really tired and I fell asleep within minutes.

Bounty

When I awoke startled by my choking on the poisonous gas. I realized that the bike went down to the surface with the poison gas all around all around me. I rummaged through my stuff as fast as I could while almost choking to death looking for my mask. When I finally found my mask, I surveyed the surroundings taking in deep breaths. Dark green vegetation and trees layered everywhere. There were ginormous birds flying everywhere squawking monsters roars. I saw trees filled with nests and animals scattering around their perfect environmental ecosystem. Not so perfect for humans like me though. A perfect place for illegal smugglers to hide from the rest of the world, if I do say so myself. I opened up the hologram map on my bike and found that I was right on top of it all! I immediately got out of the compartment and climbed back onto my bike carefully surveying my surroundings for that hill I saw earlier on the map. I spotted the area and zoomed off to the mountain as fast as I could. When I reached the top of the hill, I shut the bike off and went back to sleep this time. I awoke up a few hours later to a majestic chirping coming from birds flying overhead. "What time is it" I thought to myself. I checked my gauntlet. "8:43!" I whispered. I slept too much. I hurriedly checked my equipment. All was in good working order so I climbed out and summoned Jipsy to set up some sensors.

Bounty

"Good morning Sarah" He greeted me as he opened up before me. "Did you have a good sleep?" he asked.
"Yes" I replied in a hushed tone. "I need you to place some sensors for me." I gestured before me to direct Jipsy where to go. I referred to GPS hologram map projecting from a panel on my bike steering. I bellowed out instructions to Jipsy "Ok Jipsy what you are going to do is separate the warehouse area into 4 areas. You need to place 4 sensors within that area so when something comes I can tell its general location. Ok?" "Yes Sarah" He replied obediently. I cautioned Jipsy "You need to be cautions, there is a lot of animals around here." He responded "Affirmative"
And preceded to follow through with the plan. Given the time I wasted sleepy, I decided to set up camp immediately. I pressed a green lit button on my bike and a small tube popped out that was used originally to store extra gas, but nowadays we use antimatter to fuel everything so I retrofit the compartment to store my supplies. I took the tube and opened and unraveled the tent inside of the canister. I followed the instructions set it up while keeping one eye on the compound ahead. When Jipsy returned, I was finished pitching up the tent and I told him to 3-D map the area while I hunt for food. I summoned my (DSREP) from my gauntlet and slid it over my shoulder then pulled up the hologram on my gauntlet.

Bounty

I decided to go east and hunt those bird that chirped majestically around us when we landed on the surface earlier. The mountain was a lush green see with rocks and boulders as far as my eyes could see. Through my mask it all seemed like a blended blur. I reached the forest floor and squinted my eyes to try and get a clearer view of it all. I took a closer look at the birds flying and landing on the green marine like field. I was thinking that maybe I could pick one off and eat it when I heard a flutter. A bird fluttered before me, spinning around 180 degrees over and over again. I went into crouch and looked down sight scope of my gun, luckily I had my thermal scope on which allowed me to have a clear view of the bird through the thick fog of gas. I tracked the bird's movements to a tree where it stopped spinning and took a shot. The bird dropped to the ground silently just as predicted it would. I prayed silently, that my actions would go unnoticed. If the gang of thuds heard me they would kill me for sure. I went to retrieve the dead bird when suddenly one of the sensors Jipsy laid out went off. I immanently dropped the thought of food and made fast towards my camp and called for Jipsy. On my way back Jispy rushed beside me "the motion sensor in section 2 of the 4 North East of us went off. Shall I bring up a visual?" Said Jispy

"Yessssss, LIKE I DIDN'T KNOW THAT ALREADY" I snared sarcastically at Jipsy.

Bounty

"GO" I shrieked back at Jipsy. I don't know why this hunk of junk has to ask every time to do something. It's frustrating sometimes, especially in situations like ours now. I dogged rocks and half stumbled my way up the hill a little further. I took position at the very tip of the mountain my pulled out my rifle. I sprawled myself flat on the ground and zoomed in on my scope. I followed Jipsy's trail oh heat with my thermal scope. The trail was really bright but it was still hard see anything in my view; Jipsy gave me a report thru our com "Sarah it seems a reptilian like creature has made its way through this sector here, Shall I pursuit it and kill it?" he asked through the radio com on my gauntlet. "Yeah sure, why not ….. I, need food anyway." I replied softly. I'll let Jispy do his job, started a fire with a few twigs that were scattered around my tent and relaxed for a bit while I waited for him returned, which seemed like hours. Within that time I got to ponder on a few things, many things actually. One thought was constant and never seemed leave my mind unlike all the other aimless thoughts that came and went. Why was I so stupid to accept this mission.to assassinate an entire gang of thieves and smugglers of such high value! Why would I even think about a job that pays that much without looking at the details? The same thoughts swirled in my brain aimlessly until Jipsy came back with this huge beast that could feed hundreds starving children.

Bounty

I couldn't help smile when I saw this 9ft long bird Jipsy hovered in before me. "Plenty of meat to eat" I groaned. Although the colors of the best were green and red boldly identifying it as a predator. Not this time, I thought to myself. My mouth watered as I made my way towards the animal and I completed my thought, I can't wait to sink my teeth into that. "Drop it" I commanded Jipsy and he did so with no compliantly. "Does this fit your requirements Sarah?" Jipsy asked. His questioned made me giggle and I managed to laugh out a reply "sure does Jispy." I summoned my (RRS) and used the blade like tip to cut a piece of the bird, speared it on a stick, and placed it over the fire. Jipsy continue with the 3-D mapping while I cooked my meal already daydreaming about the savory flavor the animal will bring my taste buds. Jipsy flew away to map my requirements .When the animal was in perfect cooking condition, I cut it up with the RRS and devour the thing down to its very bare bones, I was starving. When I finished that piece, I cut another piece of the animal and another for later then disposed of the rest.

After my belly was more than overly content, I changed my cloths and was now ready for to stakeout my target thru the tonight. I planned to wait all night. Since Jipsy placed sensors all by the path multiples would go off as the targets appear I could pick them off one by one.

Bounty

You could say I was dressed in my usual tactical black with a half built ghillie suit ready for action. Sometime past before Jipsy returned and was ready to transmit the information he surveyed to my gauntlet. He did so and my gauntlet started to beep, several sensors were going off simultaneously as it downloaded all the information. The hologram displayed an array of detail about the building and its surroundings. It was a slim two story building and was hidden by the jungle like trees that surrounded the smugglers compound. The path to the warehouse seemed to wind at least 500ft and then it just disappear. The warehouse didn't have any windows or another point of entry. The only way to get in was through the front door. I could use Jipsy to cut a hole in the back of the building, but they'd notice because looking from the hologram the place looked airtight meaning that gas was not in there. Unexpectedly the trees down the path started to move... the sensors started to beep louder...my heart started to pound and raise so fast it felt like my heart would jump right out of my chest at any moment...

The anxiety clouded my judgment so much that I was second guessing my plan and I didn't know what to do… I managed to steady my nerves a bit and silence my soul long enough to think of all that could happen if things went wrong.

Bounty

There was panic inside my head, when I could finally achieve a clear strain of unclouded ideas, the first thought was to get a visual. So, I sent Jipsy to get a closer look, I quickly set up my sniper and switched thermal viewing on to take a look at what was happening on the ground below. Then with Jipsy's projected view I was able to look at the faces of my targets. I ran them through the data base and got a match almost instantly. I thought to myself, "I should take the shot, then wait for the people inside the building to come out. I guesstimated less than a few dozen would scurry about after I took my first shot (This was a real log shot guess because of the building was made out of lead and you can't use thermal viewing through lead.) I figured they would come out to check on the body and I would open fire killing the majority of them as well. I sent Jipsy down with specifics of my plan and summoned my sniper from my gauntlet once more. I position lens and zoomed in my scope accordingly. I followed the trail until I spotted someone riding a hover bike and another with an armored car. Jipsy came through the radio asking "shall I transmit feed?" "Confirmed" I responded seriously. My adrenaline went from zero to sixty miles per hour as I took aim. I went from freaking out to dead serious and I was surely hyped up. Jipsy's feed reached my gauntlet and started to run the faces of the targets below through the data base.

Bounty

Within moments we had a positive match on the driver in the armed car. I steadied my breath, and fired one-single-shot. He fell out of the side opening of the driver's seat and fell to the ground. "Yes, "clean hit "Jipsy said. The armored car came to a dead stop and several men exited the building to check on him the driver. I aimed again and scoped the faces of the men scurrying about, another positive match another shot I took and another dead…

The men began lurking about trying to figure out where the shots were coming from. I took aim at each one and fire speedily each time a matched was detected. Dead, dead and dead… The count continued 'til they smartened up began to hide behind the cars, bikes bushes.
The cars were old vehicle that still used gas and had wheels that needed changing if I'd hit them. They would have to change tires before they could come after me giving me more time to shoot. Stilly thugs, they should have used hover vehicles. Every once in a while a got a negative match and I had to find someone else to aim at, this gave them a chance to track me. This went on for what seems like a life time. Then, bingo, my scoped landed on a RED light target. The main bounty "trank him" I commanded Jispy. Jipsy loaded a tranquilizer dart and shot immediately. Our main target fell to the ground as well. "

Bounty

Hold position there" I said, and I made my way down the hill towards the compound. Jipsy bellowed out "Sarah, another caravan is making its way towards this area shall I get a visual?" "Crap" is all I could shout out. I'm going to be dead any minute if I can't get out of here. I ran to a car for some cover and put away my sniper as summoned my RRS. I cried out" YES GET A VISUAL YOU! STUPID ROBOT!!" in moments I had a visual on my RRS this time a jeep like van was making its way through the trail. It moved slowly but headed my way straight on. I was made, I had to ready my weapon for multi targets.
Jipsy's voice beckoned me with great warning "Sarah everyone in that car is a match and is of high threat." "Roger that" I scarcely replied. The car got close and my adrenalin pumped up several notches the closer it got to me. I barrel rolled out of the way of the car and I felt as if I was in a slow-motion video clip. You know, like those 20th century kids back in the day use to post on the old interface they called YOUTUBE I grew up watching as a child. Kids my age would post videos of skaters falling off railing and hurting themselves. The videos played on a continuous loop with sound effects. That's what I felt like, one fall after another on a continuous loop. I kept my eye on the scope as I tumbled.

Lastly I sighted the driver and took my shot….dead... the car spun out of control and ran into a tree close to the path by the building. I took cover behind foliage and resumed my DSREP. I zoomed out and found more targets. They were scrambling in every direction, looking for cover. I saw everything thru my thermal scope. Some were hiding behind trees, others laid suspiciously in the grass. I could tell that they were in the middle smuggling drugs, the turn over cars spewed an obvious chemical smell. I found my next target and fired with what now felt like my silent rifle of death. The first man fell to the ground with a thump. My second target didn't even know where I was shooting from so he ran into the middle of the road. A big mistake. I repositioned for the next man who was making a full sprint into the forest. Sadly for him my rifle uses high velocity pulse shots that could only be stopped if I hit at concrete or by other energy field weapon. When my last target, he tripped and ground, when he tried to get back up, I shot again and he fell once more; this time for good. While it felt like I was shooting and ducking for cover for hours, it was actually minutes before they were all dead. When I could see no one else scurry about, I paused to catch my breath. Jipsy's voice hit my ears, it felt like home, a safe haven, a sign that all was ok. "All clear… shall I continue scanning?" he said. I had never been so relieved to hear one of Jipsy's redundant question in my entire life.

Bounty

I took a few more deep breaths and his voice came thru my gauntlet again in a low digital tone, “all clear, shall I continue scanning?” he said. I scrapped myself off the ground and walked toward one of the trucks. I managed to breathe out repose to Jispy in between my troubled inhaling. “Yes, continue scanning” I reached a truck with its cargo sprawled everywhere and as I expect, the contents inside was the usual illegal chemicals. I was not surprised to see bundles of wrapped drugs. I looked around for anything of value. There wasn’t anything else of value. A couple of guns and a few bundles of rifles and packs of ammo I could salvage. I asked Jipsy to pick‘em up and bring them to my camp. I made my way to the tranquilized target Jispy managed to capture. He lay on the floor half suffocating because his mask was half off. I slapped him a couple of times to wear off some of the sedation. He awoke screaming “HELP!” I ended that cry quickly with a slight gesture of my knife. He slowly raised his hand and fixed his mask. I pointing to the warehouse and told my target “since you are going to tell me who and what is in there eventually, you may as well not waste our time and get on with it”. He unfortunately responded to my request with a great big “Like Gehgtf I will”. So, I pulled his mask off. He started to choke. I waited a few seconds and put back on. “How about now?” I asked as sarcastically as I could bare too.

Bounty

I pushed his mask again for good measure and that time he gave me the reply I wanted. "My boss, a couple of guys, and some drugs... Now please let me go." He begged.
I thought about letting him go for a second. Then said "sure, why not ". I let him get up and run away for a good thirty seconds before I shot him. Oldest trick in the book. Now it was time for the second half of this crazy ride. I proceeded to gather the bodies for a little message to the guys inside when they came out looking for their drugs… if indeed they would come out. I dragged bodies onto the path leading to the main building and laid them out in a crossed pattern. They looked like speed bumps. I was tired by the time I finished. I made my way up the hill, the sun was almost done setting. Jipsy was already at my tent floating patiently awaiting for orders. "Drop it" I commanded "and make me something to eat, get a fire going…. find the bird I sliced earlier and roast it." I walked towards my bike and pressed the button to open the sleeping compartment and climbed as Jipsy hurried off.

I woke up to the smell of food. It was the middle of the night, but I was starving. Jipsy was using his beam to turn a giant chicken looking animal that he killed for me yesterday. No doubt he used his beam to capture the bird also. THE BEAM! Of course, his has so much strength it could lift cars, I bet it could lift a few cars simultaneously.

I also think that's how he got the feathers off bird. I would have LOL but it hurt to smile, besides, I didn't care, I was hungry!! I ate quietly and in almost complete silence. I was still in that kill sort of mood, so I didn't waste time with anything. I finished up my meal and told Jipsy to make some he sweeps of the area again. He flew off and the humming of his electronics wisped me into a dead sleep.

I awoke on my own this time, no sweet smell of food and something didn't feel right. Although I went through my daily morning routine as usual, I couldn't figure out what was wrong. Jipsy came back a few minutes after I awoke and we checked on my supplies. "I found four more chicken like animals and killed them for you, I shall start the fire and cook one" Jipsy said. "All right" I responded- Wait. Wait. Wait. Did he kill things without my command? Doing so would have overridden last night's commends my. I knew he had done it. So, I slowly approached Jipsy and asked "open back hatch please" He opened the hatch. I saw nothing different. Nothing wrong from what I could see. Everything was in good working order from what I could tell. "Close it and proceed with my commands" I said. Jispy, I noticed that I said: *"with my commands"* which meant that he should carry out the command last appointed to him, which meant, I wanted nothing changed.

Bounty

I went back to my bike and open Jipsy’s digital cloud then checked the times he was active throughout the night. .He should have been active from 16:00- 21:00. But he wasn't. Instead he was active all throughout the night and the morning. I went to review last night's feed when suddenly Jipsy came up to me and said. “Sarah you will find that I was powered on throughout the night and this morning; I was performing the scan as you requested.” His whereabouts last night isn’t t what worried me. Jipsy needed to charge last night, but he didn't, that really concerned me. It’s either one of two things that he did last night. He could have returned and charged - No- that would have recorded. Or he found another source, disobeying my direct commands last night. I waved Jispy off so he can get back to cooking my meal. While I considered the two possibilities of Jipsy’s behavior last night. I had to come to some deduction reasoning quickly incase Jipsy has been pirated. I glanced back at Jipsy, his antenna was sticking straight up, and it shouldn’t be. More proof Jipsy has been tampered with. I thought about shooting him, but it took forever to upgrade him to the unit he is now. Jipsy being pirated proves that there are people in the warehouse… which means they got Jipsy, which allows them to see through his camera and see me.

I almost over looked that fact and remembered that Jipsy has live feed. I ducked for cover and summoned my DSREP to target Jipsy, I knew I would regret it that decision later, but I took the shot anyway. Jipsy sparked then fell to the ground, a few broken darts filled with liquid poured out from his exhaust fan. I heard a shot fired in the distance and I dropped to the ground instinctively, like an animal would do when a loud noise startled it. To no surprise who ever shot at me missed. It's rare to find an accurate sniper amongst known felons in this area of the surface. I returned back to see where my bike was in proximity to my current position. I quickly blasted up my thermal scope, zoomed out and looked for targets. I scanned the area and found none in my sight, I looked down towards the warehouse. I spotted someone, but without Jipsy I couldn't tell if they were legal kill. With a slight hesitation and uncertainty of legality, I took the shot anyway. Moments after the target I hit dropped, there was dead silence. I knew that I had to end this terror here and now before anyone else attacked. This left over problem was a major setback. One that limited my ability to finish this bounty fast and painless. I adjusted my gas mask, summoned my bike to follow me and headed toward the path leading to the warehouse building.

Bounty

There was still dead silence when I arrived at the roof of the warehouse looking building. I assumed that the thugs were letting me approach and preparing for my arrival. I stepped on my bike carefully, not trying to make a sound on the roof of the steel building. "I'll wait it out"
I thought to myself and took a seat on the edge of the roof. "They have to come out sometime and when they do ill have their heads." I whispered to myself. Sadly, that time would be write now because I could hear the creek of the doors open, their footsteps clambered as they ran off into the distance to escape me. They were easy targets, too easy, I set up my rifle and shot them all dead. I shot another...dead. And another. I got up and slid on the curve of the roof which resulted in me landing on a tree right off the entrance of the building. With this vantage point I got a good sight line to the majority of the building. There was at least a hundred men running around, thousands of pounds of drugs, tons of guns being tossed around, you name it, they had it. And all illegal. No wonder this job paid so much to extinguish this gang, I thought to myself as I gathered the number of targets I could hit from where I was currently positioned. I knew I could take out a few more of those guys immediately, but I decided to go scavenge one of the dead body's clothing and where them to blend into the others gang members scuffling about.

Bounty

I would slip in undetected as one of their own men. I change clothes and made my way towards the doors, I hesitated for a mere second and then continued with the plan. I ran in and yelled, "Sniper!, sniper" and continued running until I was sure that no one was concerned with me being an intruder. I swear, I never seen such a sight. All the people in the entire warehouse were gearing up. I had little time to actually survey they place, it was nothing like I had ever seen before. The warehouse was filled with 7foot tall by 7foott wide pallets of drugs. Weapons were spaced about 5feet apart from each other. Unusually neatly organized for a bunch of thugs. There were soldiers that running to and fro, most looked like poor and beaten men who lost their lives to these drugs. In the far distance, I saw a ladder leading up to a skywalk. I checked to make sure no one was following me then climbed the ladder and laid flat for a bit on the skywalk watching their movements. I figured out which one of them was in charge of this operation. It soon became clear to me that the only one dressed in red spitting out orders was the one in charge. I knew what to do "Hey what are you doing up here?" came a voice came from behind me. I stood up and looked at him, he was only a worker.

Bounty

I approached him with great speed simultaneously holstering my knife from my thigh and slit his throat. His blood dripped on my hands and onto the floor below. I had to flip his body around so he didn’t bleed everywhere and give my position away. I turned my attention back to the man in charge, took my DSREP and aimed. I waited for a clean shot and finally fired as he turned toward my direction giving orders. I missed because he shifted unexpectedly. He saw the trail of the electric pulse and looked towards me; He smiled. His odd smirk scared the hell out of me. Who has enough power and confidence to smile in the face of death? Only a powerful man could smile like when facing his enemy. He obviously has a lot more power and wit than I had anticipated. He spewed out some orders and men soon flooded towards my direction. He retreated elsewhere, but I had more immediate things to worry about. The men were in firing range and took position all around me. I made out into a sprint across the skywalk, dodging and weaving away from the lead and laser being shot at me. I was running out of walkway so I looked for a drug pile that appeared soft enough for me to dive onto. There were many to choose from and I didn't have enough time to decide which would cushion my fall best, so I just jumped off. It was at least a 12 foot drop between me and the piles.

Bounty

On my descent down I was shot in the shoulder blade. I hit feet first onto the white powdery material and jumped into a sprint towards the back of the warehouse. The men were running at a full sprint in my direction. I weaved through the organized pallets of drugs with the men following closely behind me. I removed my scope to prepare for close contact killing. I was way ahead of the men now and I could hear them yelling in the distance. I was a decent distance away close to the corner of the building. I pocketed my scope and stopped to listen. There careless scampering footsteps gave their position away…They were close. Their loud clumsy footstep came from my right. I climbed on top of a pallet and set up my sniper, using the rail as my guide to steady my shot. The man in charge came running out my way, no doubt he was trying to surprise me, but his attack was no surprise to me. I could have taken a clear shot from my sight, but he had an energy shield that covered his entire body which would have bounced my rifle's shot anywhere. You can't penetrate energy fields with energy. I had no other choice but to go loud and kill everyone off else one by one, then deal with the head honcho after. I scooted back to avoid detection and summoned my RRS. I steadied myself and gathered my thoughts as quickly as I could. Everything will change with this shot, the chance of me getting out of here alive lies solely on what I do next.

Bounty

I aimed down the barrel of my gun and shot. One more man down. He dropped before me, still alive. The entire warehouse thundered with the sounds of shots being fired. Putting my DSREP away, I kneelt down to cut some fabric off his clothes and wrapped my shoulder that still bled from the hit I took earlier. I heard more men and I readied myself. They came from the left this time. I hid behind another pallet. I left my last hit alive so the others would stop to check the body before heading my direction, distracting just long enough for me to open fire. They took the bait. I turned the corner pulled up my gun to blast them all and then I spotted the man in red. He hid behind the others. I emptied the rest of my clip into the crowd of soldiers. They all fell one by one until there was just one left. Somehow the man in red was still standing surrounded by the sea of blood from his fallen men sworn to protect him. With no ammo left in my weapon and what would take a lifetime to summon DSREP. I dropped my RRS and charged at the man in red with my knife clutched in my hand. He stood stunned while I was charging him. His stature toward me by at least 4ft. I stopped in my tracks with fear that his height may over power my might. I found myself wishing I had Jipsy to aid me. He stood tall dressed in red cargo pants and a red V-neck shirt. On his face was a powdery half-smirk that gave me chills. I could see his muscles tense up the closer I got to him.

Bounty

He made his way towards me with slow long steps. It felt like it would take forever to reach me and me him. My knife must have looked like a toothpick to him, he was so big compared to me. I set upright, frozen in fear. He was steps away from me. My body froze but my mind quickly ran the statistics in my head. He was strong and heavy, which would make him a slow heavy hitter which makes him a sloth in a fight with me. I glanced at the other dead bodies trying to find a smoke grenade or something that I can stealthy slice away at his skin. The man took his fist swing at me. I side stepped out of the way with great speed and reached one of the bodies lying on the ground. The power of his punch unsteadied him a few feet away. This gave me some time to search the bodies on the floor. He managed to keep his creepy smiles on his face while reaching for me again. My hand grabbed onto a grenade off one of the men I shot earlier. I pressed the canister button. Smoke shot out of the top covering the place in a small smoke cloud. I threw the canister at his feet and took the thermal scope out of my pocket and quickly looked through it. I saw my target clearly even though the smoke surrounded him. He was standing up looking in all directions for me. I pocketed the scope and I dashed toward him with knife in hand. I skid just slightly in front of him and slid my knife clear across his thigh causing damage to his lower thigh.

He bent over and collapsed as I ran out of his sight into the smoke cloud that surrounded us. I came back for another run at him, but he wasn't there. I my eyes quickly surveyed the room until I felt his hand land on my shoulder. He spun me around pushed my head downward and his knee hit my head with such a grand force that I actually flew a few feet back. I hit the ground and my knife spun on the floor away from me. He followed up with another punch. This time he hit my jaw so powerful I was shocked my teeth didn't fly out of my mouth. Disorientated a bit, I reached for the RRS but I failed to grab it. I then remembered the first time I used the techno gauntlet. I summoned the DSR out of a man's hand once. It turned into its 3-D plain inside of him. I mustered up as much energy as I could and lunged my fist into his chest and pressed the button on my gauntlet that summoned my rifle. The square cube popped up, and formed into my 3-D plain riffle impaling the man's chest. His chest opened up and he fell down the ground in pain and gasping for air. He tried reaching for something that wasn't there. I looked at his face to see that I have defeated him. He didn't have that smug face anymore. I pulled the rifle out of his chest. The rifle was covered in the man's blood and pieces of fell off. I put the barrel to his head, smiled with the same ridiculous smirk he gave me and ended his life proudly. It took a few minutes before I heard more men making their way to us.

Bounty

I started to load my RRS. The footsteps came fast so I put everything away except for my knife. I thought I'd hide among the dead and silently kill each and every one of them till I completed the mission. The men came closer. They hovered right on top of me. My first kill was a short man who looked bit scared at the site of all the blood. I got up and dashed at him, I slip the back of his neck and dropped to the floor concealing myself underneath him. The other men turned around. They scanned the area with their rifles, poking dead bodies and checking them for signs of life. One man came close to me and I killed him like the first guy. This time the others saw him fall. The three men left approached his body. They gathered around him and looked over the body. I stood up like a ghost behind them and lunged at them. One man spotted me and turned in my direction, he aimed his rifle but I was already close enough to nock his rifle out of his hands. I spun up a 180 spin and lodged my knife in his throat. I pulled my knife out and then spotted the last two men standing. They had the expression of children that just saw the scariest thing alive. They were both shaking, unwilling to pull up their guns and shoot. They slowly started stepping to back. I opened my RRS and loaded 2 shots. "Go!!!!" I shouted "there's no point of killing yawl, so go" I said. The men turned to walk away and I shot twice. Classic way to kill someone.

Bounty

I saw it in a movie once. I continued to load my RRS when My ID card began to make sounds. I pulled it out of my pocket to see why it was going haywire and the darn thing congratulated me. It thanked me for eliminating the threat and that drones were dispersed to identify the kills. My progress and footage will be used to persuade people to check out the bounty board. Then it transferred 6,000,000,000 into my account. I had just single handedly eliminated the largest smugglers known and they are using my victory to advertise for more hits on their site. One thing my card did not do or imply, is what they're going to do with all those weapons and drugs left behind!

www.ingramcontent.com/pod-product-compliance
Ingram Content Group UK Ltd.
Pitfield, Milton Keynes, MK11 3LW, UK
UKHW041901190726
13854UKWH00003B/1025

9 781312 878747